Look at Drip's beak in these sketches — just like a duck's.

Here is a very early sketch of Drip. He hasn't got any scales! What else is different?

He has a little crest in this sketch.

This is how Drip turned out in the end . . .

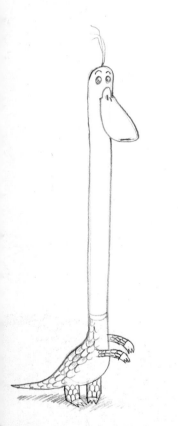

Imagine if Drip had ended up with a long neck, just like a giraffe.

This sketch looks quite similar to the final Drip, but there are still a few differences. How many can you spot?

Which one is your favourite?

A Note from the Author

The idea of a dinosaur egg hatching out in the wrong nest had been in my mind for years before I actually wrote *Tyrannosaurus Drip*. At first I planned for two eggs to be swapped, and that the two baby dinosaurs would become friends even though their families hated each other – a bit like Romeo and Juliet! But then I thought that might be a bit corny, so I decided there would be just one egg.

Next I had to think of a trick for Drip to play, and I came up with the idea that he could trick the tyrannosaurus family with their own reflections in a river. But that meant that the duckbill dinosaurs and the tyrannosauruses would have to live on different sides of the river. How would the duckbill egg start on one side and travel to a nest across the river? That kept me awake for a while until I dreamed up the compsognathus: she could steal the egg and swim with it. That solved the problem and I was ready to go.

Once I started writing I realised I wanted a kind of chorus, so I introduced the dinosaur chants. When I act out the story on the stage I get the audience to recite the duckbill chants – and I give someone the special job of hatching out the dinosaur egg!

My son Alastair is very good at acting poor little Drip, but the trouble is that his daughter Poppy sometimes cries when she sees the tyrannosauruses being mean to him, so I can't cast Alastair too often.

If you'd like some hints on acting out the story at home or in a classroom, you could take a look at www.picturebookplays.co.uk, which is a website I created when I was the Children's Laureate and which has lots of ideas for dramatising picture books. You can even see a video of a class performing Tyrannosaurus Drip.

Of course the story wouldn't be the same without David Roberts's wonderful pictures. I love how David uses cool greens for the duckbills and orange and reds for the T Rexes, and the way he has given the T Rex mum an overlapping top jaw while the dad's bottom jaw sticks out. He's a very thoughtful and clever illustrator.

So I'd like to thank David, and also to wish Tyrannosaurus Drip a happy tenth birthday.

Julia Donaldson

JULIA DONALDSON   DAVID ROBERTS

TYRANNOSAURUS DRIP

MACMILLAN CHILDREN'S BOOKS

In a swamp beside a river, where the land was thick with veg,
Lived a herd of duckbill dinosaurs who roamed the water's edge.

And they hooted, "**Up with rivers!**" and they hooted, "**Up with reeds!**"

And they hooted, "**Up with bellyfuls of juicy water weeds!**"

Now across the rushy river, on a hill the other side,

Lived a mean Tyrannosaurus with his grim and grisly bride.

And they shouted, "Up with hunting!" and they shouted, "Up with war!"

And they shouted, "Up with bellyfuls of duckbill dinosaur!"

But the two Tyrannosauruses, so grisly, mean and grim,

Couldn't catch the duckbill dinosaurs because they couldn't swim.

And they muttered, "Down with water!" and they muttered, "Down with wet!"

And they muttered, "What a shame that bridges aren't invented yet."

Now a little Compsognathus (but for short we'll call her Comp)
Found a duckbill egg and stole it from a nest beside the swamp.

And she swam with it,

and ran with it,

And murmured, "Clever me!"
And, "Won't the baby Comps be thrilled
with duckbill egg for . . .

"...T!"

She dropped the egg in terror
  and went running for her life
From the mean Tyrannosaurus
  and his grim and grisly wife.

And the duckbill egg went rolling, and at last it came to rest
In – of all unlikely places – the Tyrannosaurus nest.

Now the mother T had great big jaws
   and great enormous legs,
But her brain was rather little
   and she couldn't count her eggs.
And she sang, "Hatch out, my terrors,
   with your scaly little tails
And your spiky little toothies
   and your scary little nails."

Out hatched Babies One and Two,
    as perfect as could be,
But Mother T was horrified by
    Baby Number Three.
And she grumbled, "He looks weedy,"
    and she grumbled, "He looks weak."
And she grumbled, "What long arms –
    and look, his mouth is like a beak!"

"He just needs feeding up," said Dad
 and gave the babes some meat.
The first two gulped and guzzled
 but the third refused to eat.
And he said, "I'm really sorry,"
 and he said, "I simply can't."
And he said, "This meat looks horrible.
 I'd rather eat a plant."

"A PLANT!" yelled Mum in horror, and Dad said, "Get a grip!"

His sisters found a name for him: "Tyrannosaurus Drip!"

And they shouted, "Up with hunting!" and they shouted, "Up with war!"

And they shouted, "Up with bellyfuls of duckbill dinosaur!"

Poor Tyrannosaurus Drip tried hard to sing along

But the others yelled, "You silly drip, you've got the words all wrong!"

For he hooted, "Down with hunting!" and he hooted, "Down with war!"

And he hooted, "Down with bellyfuls of duckbill dinosaur!"

Drip's sisters soon grew big enough to hunt with Dad and Mum
But they turned on Drip and told him, "You're not fierce enough to come."

And he cried, "They've gone without me!" and he cried, "Alackaday!"
And he cried, "This doesn't feel like home. I'm going to run away!"

So he ran off to the river, where he saw a lovely sight:

A herd of duckbill dinosaurs, all hooting with delight.

And they hooted, "**Up with rivers!**" and they hooted, "**Up with reeds!**"

And they hooted, "**Up with bellyfuls of juicy water weeds!**"

As he stood there on the bank, a sudden urge took hold of him,

And he jumped into the water . . . and discovered he could SWIM!

And the duckbills came to greet him by the rushy river's edge

And they hooted, "Nice to see you!" and they hooted, "Have some veg!"

And Drip, who was delighted that they hadn't run away,

Ate bellyfuls of water weeds, and played with them all day.

Then he gazed into the river and he asked them, "Who, oh who

Is that creature in the water?" And they laughed and said, "It's you!"

That night the lightning crackled

and a storm blew down a tree.

And it fell across the river,

and the Ts cried out, "Yippee!"

And they shouted, "Up with hunting!"
and they shouted, "Up with war!"
And they shouted, "Up with bellyfuls
of duckbill dinosaur!"

Drip's sisters stepped onto the bridge, but then began to frown,

For there in front of them stood Drip, who yelled, "Look out! Look DOWN!"

And they looked into the water, and they each let out a yelp,
And one cried, "Water monsters!" And the other one cried, "HELP!"

Their mother scolded, "Nonsense!"
    and she joined them on the tree.
Then she looked into the water and
    exclaimed, "Good gracious me!"

The three of them stood trembling,
    and Dad said, "Get a grip!
You're all of you as drippy as
    Tyrannosaurus Drip!"

He strode onto the bridge
    and scoffed,
"I bet there's nothing there."
Then he looked into the water —

and he **jumped** into the air.

And how the duckbills hooted when he landed with a crash,
And the tree bridge broke . . .

. . . and four

Tyrannosauruses went

SPLASH!

And spluttering, and clinging to
the branches of the tree,
They went whooshing down a waterfall
and all the way to sea.

And the duckbills hooted happily: they hooted, "Hip hip hip . . .
Hooray for the heroic, one-and-only Duckbill Drip!"